JAMES COWAN

THE BOOK OF LETTERS

A meditation on the alphabet

Balgo Hills
Publishing

James G. Cowan (1942 - 2018) is the author of more than thirty books of fiction, non-fiction, poetry, art monographs, and philosophy. He is a recipient of the Australian Literary Society's Gold Medal for his novel A Mapmaker's Dream, as well as an honorary doctorate in the USA. He holds a Ph.D. for his biography Hamlet's Ghost. His books have been published in over twenty languages.

James valued literature not just as a challenging form of expression, but as a way of celebrating and enhancing our perceptions in a rapidly changing world.

CONTENTS

INTRODUCTION

The alphabet is the oldest form of expression that we know. That it is derived from Phoenician letters and Egyptian hieroglyphics does not suggest its antiquity is any less for being so. Their letters are largely grounded in images, and therefore they are a pictorial representation of sounds that the mouth utters. Latin letters, however, have lost their formal imagery in the interest of conciseness. They have become signs whose origin eludes the eye, so that words might be more perfectly articulated and expressed.

The beauty of the alphabet is that it allows us to think on paper. All the dream-like abstractions of our brains are given the opportunity to emerge as words, and so allow thought to attain to a tangible form. Each letter, when it enters a word, intimates a meaning. And to express meaning is the primary reason why humankind exists in the first place. We are, so to speak, *homo logos* – that is, we are a species determined by the power of reason and its dependence upon formal expression.

We take the alphabet for granted. All twenty-six letters are viewed as a means to an end. They do not represent themselves but are servants of the words that they enact. When the word 'live' is written down, for example, we accept it as a verb or condition of existence that signifies something to do with being alive. We do not look at its letters as such, but at the thought the word represents. And yet, if we re-arranged these letters, the words 'a veil' suddenly appear. Then we must ask ourselves: have its letters imposed another, altogether secret meaning upon our thoughts?

Is it, perhaps, that being 'alive' is a veil concealing the fact of our origin in matter? It may be that its letters have found a way to suggest the beauty of our agglomeration as beings. We are salts and trace elements arranged in such a way as to intimate a life. And yet this side of our being is 'veiled', so to speak, simply because we do not notice it. The esoteric nature of letters has thus been diminished. We are content to accept our physical nature as living beings, without acknowledging how en-veiled we might actually be. Indeed, it might be that words conceal what we are to ourselves.

Ever since I was a child I have been enamoured by letters and words. I can remember writing my very first word as a four or five year-old. The word I wrote on the page that day at school with my pencil was that of 'said'.

Not 'say' in the present tense, but rather the past tense of utterance. Things were 'said' and therefore existed. It was my first encounter with the primacy of being lying at the heart of letters and words. The alphabet had become a living reality to me.

It was not until I heard my first metaphor while out hunting rabbits with my father that I understood the power of language. He informed me, after shooting a rabbit, that the poor creature was "as dead as a doornail." My childish thoughts then had to grapple with the idea that death and a doornail were unaccountably drawn into a particular association. It was hard for me to fathom. Language had distorted death and given it substance. Now it was a doornail. My father's remark had alerted me to the idea that there might be an inbuilt play element behind words.

So words, indeed language, is a game. It plays with us as much as we play with it. To take words at their face-value is to reduced their implication. Something that is dead has been reduced to a flatness, almost and abstraction. But when it is compared to a doornail, the mind becomes enlivened. It can see a nail in an old wooden door with a coat hanging from it. Suddenly the death of that rabbit has spread out by association into another order of expression. I have never forgotten that rabbit. It lies on the ground as a perfect representation of the deadness of a nail.

The word 'said' and the metaphor 'dead as a doornail' became my introduction to letters and language. It became, too, the turning-point in my life. Words as play I now understood to be a way forward into the essence of meaning. I was no longer a mute thing, a flower or tree perhaps, but a person who could summon up meaning from the mere arrangement of letters on a page. It was a revelation to me. In those youthful moments I became a logomath. I had unlocked the door to that treasury we know as creative expression.

The alphabet, however, I still considered to be no more than a tool, a vehicle. It merely served a purpose. I had never considered the arrangement of letters on the page as anything other than the substance of a word. They did not speak for themselves. They were not even the washed-out remnants of such images as lion, hand, chick, or falcon that we see in hieroglyphs. It was if they had become denuded of their origins. All antiquity and ageless thought that lay behind each letter as developed by my ancient forbears had been lost.

It meant of course that the abstraction of letters took precedence over any meaning that they might conceal. There was never any sense that such letters might house a numinosity not immediately evident. In other words, that there might be a system of metaphysics lying, unnoticed, below the surface of every word. Even my knowledge of how tribal people think inside their myths did not register with me as to the value of words being, in some way, numinous artifacts. That myths might conceal a metaphysical language, rather than simply a place to store cultural lore and knowledge, was the last thing I had thought about.

The alphabet had not registered with me as a repository of mysterious emblems. I use these words advisably. There is something emblematic about all our letters. They range across our thoughts, whether we can see them or not, as a strange ethereal consequence. It takes a superior mind to know this, even if he or she merely writes them down or uses them as utterance. A tribal person will tell you that if a word is misspoken, then it has lost its power. A misspelt word is thus a piece of dust. The sound of the spoken voice must therefore carry the veracity of true expression, otherwise it is lost.

Which brings me back to those twenty-six letters. I think of the Phoenicians and the Greeks struggling to break away from the organic nature of Egyptian hieroglyphs. They no longer wanted to see the letter A as an ox's head, or Q as a hilly slope. What appeared as words as images in the tombs of Egypt was too elaborate for them. They needed something more concise, a system of signs that expressed all they thought with brevity – and not, as the Chinese do even to this day with their characters, as pictorial impressions. Sounds needed to be tamed and not allowed to run around as a menagerie of images only.

So that the modern Latin alphabet, which we use today, has undergone a civilizing process. It is no longer a wild, natural thing known only to those temple scribes with their papyrus and nibs. To walk into a tomb in Upper Egypt, even now, is to be confronted by words as formalized images. They are a delight to the eye, of course. But are they capable of expressing abstract thought in the way we understand it? The Egyptian Book of the Dead may well be one long metaphor about death and dying, but is it in itself a clearly articulated metaphysic drawn from abstract thought? I cannot answer that question because I am not an ancient Egyptian priest. But I suspect it does not.

Let it be said, then, that letters live their own life. In spite of their seeming passivity, there is something spiky and intrusive about their formation. They are not just squiggles or curvy lines. What each letters seems to say to us is this: use me but be careful of your intent. Do not think that what I contain, that numinous substrate from which I am made, will enliven your words unless you respect what I represent. I am the building-block of words, of language, the very heart of the expression that you struggle to realize.

It is at this point that we begin to gain a new respect for the alphabet. All those twenty-six letters are foot soldiers defending the high hill of expression. They are marshaled on the field of battle where war between thought and clear intent is being waged. Some might die in the process; but their martyrdom gives us new insight into the power of language as a victory over muteness or muddled thinking. We must see every one of these letters as well-armoured signs that spell out the possibility of extending our victory over the natural passivity of consciousness itself.

So that the alphabet is more than a verbal tool. It is, if the truth be known, the finest construct that the human mind has yet devised. Without it we can only talk, create myths and stories, and ritualize these in dance or song. We have no way of preserving them other than through memory, recital, and enactment. In all of these activities, however, letters do not exist. They might lie about as shadows, as shades almost, lurking in the spoken word, but they do not attain to their own specific density as words preserved on paper. Their explosive qualities are thus transient because of their ephemeral nature. It is only when they are placed on paper that we can begin to analyze their metaphysical properties or observe their spiritual nature. Is this possible, one might ask? Do letters have spiritual attributes? These questions were addressed a long time ago by a group of thinkers from Moorish Spain, in cities such as Cordoba and Zaragoza, as well in other places, Basra and Baghdad, for example. Between the tenth and thirteenth centuries in particular, men struggled to uncover the hidden properties of letters. Letters, they argued, are the secret utterance of God.

In Arabic the science of the unseen and the science of manifestation are represented by the letter 'ayn', which means 'eye'. Letters, therefore, house an esoteric meaning as well as their capacity to represent. Men such as Ibn Masarra, Ibn Arabi, Ibn Gabirol, Al Tirmidhi, and At-Tustari spent much of their lives exploring the mystical properties of letters in their bid to understand those revelations inherent in their sacred texts. They wanted to plumb the depths of the Koran and the Torah. They were not satisfied that everything on the surface was all that the text contained. The science of primordality and that of pre-ordained destinies became their ultimate quest.

These men were driven to see mystically through letters. To them, every word (and by implication, every letter) possessed a light. When a meaning is truly grasped, then the light of the intellect shines forth. As Al-Tirmidhi remarked, "Words are containers, and the lights are the stuff with which these containers are filled." By visualizing the 'lights' within each letter, within each word, a man could enter a courtyard where the primacy of mystical insight might finally be observed.

Everything that is subject to thought calls for indication. To Ibn Masarra, the world in its entirety is a book whose letters are the speech of God. The world with all its creatures and signs make up a ladder which a person must climb in order to discover what is forever veiled. God manifests Himself through language, the language of signs, which is the natural world married to language. Nature speaks to us, and we heed its call, but only when we articulate its message. It is at this point that letters and words come into their own. We call them forth from matter so that matter itself might be given a voice.

Matter is entirely restricted until it is called forth into language. When we name a thing we give it form. No one knows when this first event happened, other than to posit the idea that when a grunt was transformed into an action or a thing, then a word was uttered for the first time. Who spoke that first word? No one knows. All we do know is that the long road from grunt to formal expression spelt the beginning of humankind as a linguistic species. We were now animals under the spell of words. Out of the vast store of particles that make up matter a rudimentary intellect had begun to emerge.

At the heart of this process is language and letters.

We will never knows how this came about, but we do sense some kind of miracle has occurred. Why should words impose themselves on matter? It is a mystery that these medieval Moorish philosophers struggled to unravel.

They recognized that though Mohammad could not read or write, he had found a way to articulate a revelation. But it could never be a revelation until scribes wrote it down and arranged it as the Koran. Text thus represents the solidification of utterance; words on paper carry the message of divine affinities masquerading as the arrangement of letters. Which draws us back into the mysterious properties of the alphabet. It has become, as the ancients well knew, the beginning of a journey into the miracle of being itself.

I make these observations not only because I am a writer, but because my early encounter with a dead rabbit urged me to put aside my eyes as the sole arbitrator of existence. Seeing is not always believing, I told myself. The Moorish philosophers of old had taught me to assume that words are not enough. If there are 'lights' inside words, then it was up to me to find a way to call forth this light through a new respect for letters. I had to allow the alphabet to talk to me. I had to see each letter not as a sophisticated glyph, but as a sign without similitude. Letters, I had to accept, were flawless indications of the noblesse of being itself.

It is the journey I am making now as I write this introduction. I am, in very real a sense, entering each word as a repository of revelation not unlike Muhammad when he sat down after one of his visionary encounters to recount what he had witnessed. It may be true of John of Patmos, too, when he wrote his Gospel and his masterful Apocalypse. We sense in both these texts a mind in thrall to the revelationary nature of the Word. He had found a way to harness letters to the pure 'lights' of his intellect. No wonder his words are so timelessly incandescent; they harbour spiritual properties that only a man of high intent could possibly arrange.

It is well to consider further these 'lights' that seemingly reside, like a chrysalis inside a cocoon, at the heart of letters. As an amateur etymologist, I am trying to discover whether there might an inner core of collusion between the letters of the alphabet and the sense of enclosure that they represent. Do letters, when they are fashioned into words, offer a plurality of secrets that suggest their origin in pre-existence? Certainly our Moorish philosophers thought so as they went about the business of transforming them into transcendent entities.

No one did this better than Ibn Arabi. He took the letter *waw,* for example, and released its 'lights' as a sanctified image for men to contemplate. He was not satisfied with its surface value as a letter; rather, he wanted it to project onto the screen of our minds a kind of puppet theatre of meanings that reflected the essential soul of such a letter. Thus the letter waw, spelt as w-a-w, joins together the waw of ibseity, of absolute fullness, with the help of the alif (A) the purest of all letters, to the waw of cosmic existence. In so doing, it becomes the premier letter of transcendent life. "Waw is the noblest of letters which carries within in a multitude of aspects and precious applications," he wrote. This was his way of saying that each letter has a cosmic intelligence all of its own.

How can one begin to understand what Ibn Arabi means unless we cast aside the letter as being merely a sign? Clearly he regarded waw as a luminous letter, one whose matrices illuminated creation. The interiority of letters, he believed, corresponds to the Divine Mystery. World-beginning thus becomes manifest in the articulation of language as an adjunct of the Word. Not only does it take in air as part of its substance, as in speech, but it also enters into ink and the book, and so becomes solidified as text.

The hiddenness of a letter then reveals itself in observable, physical form on the page. Waw becomes the essence of light as a manifestation of Divine Light.

It is at this point that we begin to understand how there is a metaphysic in language and in the letters that conscribe it. Letters and language are far more than a form of thought, a way of delineating the way we think. When words appear on pillars in ancient Egypt, or great slabs of Akkadian stone in Mesopotamia, we are at once made aware of language and letters as an enhancement to architecture. They become decorations, but not in any way superficial or titillating; rather, they inaugurate mute stonework, make it more complete.

One never thinks of language as a physical artifice, except when it appears in Irish illuminated script, the *Book of Kells* for example. Those medieval monks clearly regarded each word of God as an illumination in the same way as Al Tirmidhi and Ibn Arabi did when they spoke about the 'lights' within letters. For Ibn Masarra also, the letter A (alif) possesses five faculties: that of intellect, memory, understanding, thought, and imagination. They enhance meaning just as hieroglyphs enhance architecture. Thus the 'lights' within letters is their capacity to illuminate meaning in a way that ordinary thought does not.

I find this an interesting concept: that words are capable of decorating our lives. We wade into their meaning whenever we regard them as being more than just script on the page. The page, parchment or papyrus, of course, are their backdrop, and the pen is the baton that orchestrates their creation. Ink, because of its blackness, enlivens them, makes them blossom on the page. Whether it is the first word in St. Luke's Gospel in the *Book of Kells* depicting a vast floor-plan complete with wall niches and mandalas, or an elaborate teardrop motif containing the words of a poem in the form of a knot on a wall in Konya, or a finely patterned design of Kufic script inside the Alhambra Palace, we are at once made aware of words as decoration.

Chinese characters, too, display this same sense of interrelation between form and content. All of nature is implicit in every letter, it seems. The word 'east', for example, is depicted as the sun rising behind a tree. 'Man' is a stylized walking strophe. And 'horse' is depicted as a four-legged animal with a proud mane and head. Chinese characters unfold vertically, from the top to the bottom, imitating the movement of a theogeny descending from heaven to earth. In contrast, Arabic script proceeds horizontally, on the plane of becoming. It starts on the right, which is the field of action, and moves towards the left, which is the region of the heart.

All of which gives rise to the most beautiful of all decorations, the arabesque. We find in the interlacing of animals on the *Book of Darrow* or the animaline decorations in the *Lindisfarne Gospels* intimations of letters and words as suggestive as any hieroglyph in the *Book of the Dead*. What can we deduce from such decoration, this glory of the arabesque? Only that words yearn to attain to a beauty at the hands of a craftsman. At the same time, they want to destroy the inveterate logic of classification as mere abstraction.

Letters, therefore, have a kind of patina to them. Inbuilt into their formation is the notion of grains in wood, especially when they are able to capture shadows on a temple pillar. We at once recognize that they possess a liveliness that words on a page do not. It is noteworthy that the Egyptian cartouche, which is a stylized oval-shaped design enclosing the name of a Pharaoh, blends the idea of 'circuit' or 'ring' what, in ancient Egyptian, became the word for 'name'. A cartouche was thus a naming emblem with a definite form to it. Words had become encased.

Indeed, in ancient times, words accompany images as a part of their overall design. Words were not allowed to depart from the image; instead they became the framework surrounding those scenes of the afterworld in a Pharaoh's tomb. Standing before such a tableau, one is drawn into the subliminal articulation of sublime events as pictorial method. Osiris on his death barge is accompanied by a swathe of words. Such is the beauty of the cartouche and hieroglyph: it demands of us to put aside rational thought and plunge into the strange plethoral nature of the word.

I am beginning to ask myself where all this is leading. I have broken away from the straightforward expression of the twenty-six Latin letters of our alphabet in my journey into the realms of architecture, wall decoration, arabesques, and illuminated Gospels. Suddenly these letters have been released from their carapace of conciseness, at least to my mind. Where will they take me? Will I be able to keep up with their wanderings across the pages of my thoughts?

Already, it seems, I have begun to ascribe to the quiet insouciance of a temple scribe pondering his hieroglyphs. I have allowed letters to begin to animate me.

This is where the alphabet leads us. Letters offer us a true metaphysics of language. There is none other than an esoteric meaning hidden to the ordinary understanding in each letter. Letters do not reveal their true nature unless a reader is of pure intent. As Ibn Arabi relates, "This science of letters is truly a sublime station that confers the divine knowledge of Being." Ibn Masarra further emphasized that it is not about providing practical applications or powers to letters, but of penetrating the mystical meanings buried in each one of them. As the Vedas also suggest, there is a deep encoding in words and letters that transcends their overt, physical reality.

This is the beginning of our foray into the mystery of letters. With them we are able to create metaphors, the chief substance of nature and of language. Poetry is established through metaphors, which are drawn from the arrangement of letters. What letters do is compound words, which in turn produce metaphors. The best poetry, as we know, deals not only with natural images but with lofty thoughts, those spiritual suggestions and obscure relations. Is it not true that when we look at a Japanese scroll containing no more than a few words depicted as characters, we shiver with anticipation? They have reached out to us with their secret encodement.

The book and the cosmos are the same. He who is a true interpreter externalizes the universe in his contemplation and articulation of the word. The link between man's intent and the word is crucial: a word that is not performed or written 'correctly' loses its power, as we have already observed. Only when reflection, remembrance, and inner vision are practiced can the true essence of a word be realized. In doing so, they become a part of the warp and woof of the world. It is no accident that I allude to weaving, because we often refer to words as 'weaving' their magic on our thoughts and our imagination.

Opaqueness is at the heart of all letters. They do not reveal their inner core so easily. The act of penetration on our part is an act of solidarity with them. Why this should be so is a mystery which our Moorish philosophers tried to address by way of exploring their esoteric properties. They, like me, were logomaths, but working under entirely different circumstances. The logos in letters, their inner rationality, is for them an experiment in the domain of free-ranging meanings. A letter is a dolmen of hidden sense rising above the amorphous nature of nature and of matter. It is an incarnation bound to a metaphysic.

Thus, my relationship to letters must be more than functional. I can no longer treat them simply as signs. In doing so, I am treating language as a mere adjunct to thought and not a spontaneous eruption of inner significations that partakes of metaphysics. The converse to functionality is invocation: words and letters are designed to predicate meaning as being the hidden consciousness of the cosmos. They 'summon up' the source of primordial experience that defies analysis.

Fidelity is the essence of letters. When a letter expresses itself as a labial or palatal, there is intimation of their essence. We breathe out words. They are empty of objectivity save as ideation. No one can 'see' a word except as an expression of letters on paper. When we hear them, it is a different process than when we 'see' them on a page. If for Al Tirmidhi they might contain 'lights', for others they then become the perfect embodiment of a density that we associate with the real. A word becomes a thing by association, no more. It remains true to that association, of course, through an act of fidelity. *Fide*, truth, makes up the structure of every letter in the alphabet.

So far I have not considered the emergence of letters and their relation to time. Time is a contingency, and I have already suggested that letters are timeless. How can I say this when I know that they are formulated and devised? They have emerged out of visual activity, a sense of connection, between an object (ox) and a designation, the letter A. Seeing a thing, an object, and devising a letter from it may have been an exceedingly slow activity in time, but it was also a spontaneous event. The object was finally subsumed by a letter to reveal something timeless: that is, writing as an ever evolving and eternal act of the Universal Mind.

Nor have I considered the alphabet as a form of ascetical practice. In other words, that letters have been reduced to principial values which extend beyond their applications. In a strange way, I can visualize a word as a demonstration of such an ascetic condition. Words are stripped of their grammar to become shimmering bodies of ascetical fervor.

What do I mean by this remark? That a word is a kind of cave into which we enter in order that we might experience a stillness and a state of certitude. In this cave a word becomes a modality of being in which truth is enshrined. In the ascetic word divinity is realized as a timeless vibration that irradiates the universe.

Could it be that the ascetic nature of letters is determined by their solitude? Letters live in and of themselves. They are never relative to one another except as the designation we call the alphabet. L and T, for example, are not remotely akin to one another; they function in isolation only. Yet when a word is written down most of the letters in the alphabet, if not all, lose their identities as expressed by the mouth. Their 'sound' is subsumed by the need to work together. It is at this moment that a letter quits its cave and becomes a member of a community. It is not longer ascetical, but parenthetical.

The alphabet, as a communion of letters, then becomes a formula for definition. It helps us to define reality. Until that moment reality has no meaning: it is merely a suggestion of thingness. Letters, indeed words, provide us with the ability to sound out reality as a presence within ourselves. They allow us to absorb the world. Without the alphabet, the thingness of the world would be incapable of definition. The alphabet, therefore, is a mediator between thought and thing: each letter contributes value to the overall composition of the cosmos.

Which suggests that letters and words possess a cosmological significance. They inhabit the domain of metaphysics whereby thingness is raised to another order of being. A word denotes a pristine condition, a reality that is entirely of this world – and yet, equally, not of this world. Christ's remark to the effect that man does not live by bread alone speaks to the essentially metaphysical nature of being, which transcends thingness, a condition that he fully recognized. Letters and words act as a bridge between the finite and the infinite, between bread and the Logos.

The solitude of the letter is therefore ameliorated by the word. It joins with other letters in the pursuit of meaning. By way of comparison letters could be likened to atoms. Though they swirl around in isolation, indiscriminate and yet energized, they come together to form a word in order to flesh out the reality of a thing. To exist quickly becomes an amalgam of letters. We do not actually live unless we are lettered. A tree does not exist as such until it is named. Naming a tree is our way of providing it with identity.

Clearly letters are linked to the idea of identity.

They behold things. Beholding is a part of their nature. To be-hold is to, metaphysically at least, encusp reality, give it substance. As atoms come together to create molecules, so do letters combine to form words. It is this coming together that is a beholding. Conversely, without letters there can never be a beholding. This is why it was important for humankind to fashion language, letters, and words. They became, for the cosmos, the guardians of the principle of beholding.

We can say, then, that language allows us to behold. It enables us to frame the world. No other creature is capable of such a beholding, not even apes. They might encounter the world through their senses, but that does not mean that they understand it. It is only words that make it possible for us to understand reality. And in such a process letters have a vital role to play. They emerge from their solitude to provide a platform for understanding. Understanding and meaning are a part of their molecular behavior.

I have written the Book of Letters with the intention of allowing letters to reveal their secret life by way of a free-ranging association of images. It occurred to me that letter have been left to live in a shadowy world of abstraction for too long. They exist only as signs, as little else. I needed to find a way to release them from such a constraint. The Moorish philosophers of old attempted to do the same when they credited letters with esoteric properties, as well as the beauty and precision of number symbolism, which came to them via Pythagoras. Jewish philosophers further perfected this system when they created the Cabbala in Spain. Numbers and inner meaning were finally placed in the service of letters so that they might act as filigree on the surface of reality.

Ibn Masarra argued that when a thing is summoned to 'Be!' (kun) through the act of saying, its isness is finally established as a form. It has become detached from the All. This spiritual form is the word fashioned so that a thing might be. It is the true essence of the thing that comes into being. Letters, he maintained, contain a vibration that needs to be accessed. If we allow letters to become the slaves of words, their numinous properties will forever lie in abeyance. That is, remain shackled.

I wanted to free letters from such slavery. How could I bring them to life as emblems of their own intrinsic verticality? In the beginning I thought it an impossible task. Latin script, as I have already alluded to, is certainly rather graphic and formularized, not at all like cuneiform, Kufic letters, hieroglyphs or Chinese characters. Their design is very distant from the things that underpin their origin. It was clear that I had to find a way to allow them to announce themselves through their use in words.

Right use of metaphor, simile, and free-ranging association was the only way I thought possible to allow them to 'decorate' our thoughts and imagination. In a sense, the screen of our mind needed to become the equivalent of temple pillars or a dome of script gracing a mosque. Letters and words needed to display their dexterity with the fulsomeness of images or the wisdom inherent in Celtic knots on a page. Nothing should prevent words becoming celestial images in the same way as Carolingian letters impose their majesty upon us. When the calligraphist Jamal al-Din Yaqut informs us of a scribe "whose script was beautiful", I realized how important it was to express the essence of Latin letters as 'beautiful objects' through the medium of the poetic image alone.

The Book of Letters represents an attempt to devise a mental calligraphy that does full justice to the genius of our letters. It is hoped that by encouraging each letter of the alphabet to speak freely to us we might begin to understand how a 'metaphysics of language' really works. Is it possible to resuscitate the way we perceive and think by allowing letters to reveal their inner life? I certainly hope so. It is for this reason that I offer a meditation upon each of the twenty-six letters in the alphabet. They are the beginning of a process of rethinking how we deal with the world, with our own subjectivity, and with the possibility of rejuvenating language itself.

Let us begin this journey into the alphabet in a spirit of reverence for the genius of letters. They bear a hidden image, a hidden meaning, and a hidden truth deep within their construct. When men first devised them they did so because they believed that God alone had directed them to that end. In a sense, they had become co-workers and blacksmiths in the foundry of the Logos. They were logosthetes in the service of the word. Precision was their watchword.

THE BOOK OF LETTERS

Letters are an uncompounded spiritual power,
the foundation of all things.

Abd Allah ibn Masarra

... is a crooked road. It inspires nullity, the wandering life of aspiration and discipline. He who adopts this letter as his talisman is in league with the god of wayfarers, the boundary stone, as well as that line of limit between this world and the next. N is a self- noughting of spurious reality, the dark reaches of obscurity. It falls back upon itself and then darts upward, ever exploring the roof of the mouth as a palatal. Who knows where it will take us? Nascent letter, it is born of escape. Of course, it has its critics who dislike its peripatetic ways. The tail of the dragon, glowing in its intent, suggests the luminosity of its diatribe when it flicks back and forth. It argues with itself, always reviewing its response, hoping to abandon the rigidity of its acutely rendered angles. Become a straight line! it seems to say. Or enter into the formulations of a bird's wing whereby bending to the suscitation of the wind is the norm. N is all about ascent; it wants to release itself from the temerity of earth. Nothing stands between it an its perpendicular ways.

... is the cave, the well, the maw. It is a receptacle of sage attributes. No one knows where it might lead: an underground stream filled with the quiet voice of antique waters. It requires lips of an all-encompassing nature to announce its name. O is One, the primordial moment, the cosmos in a state of fecund order on a Japanese scroll that signals the enormous O of All. Who cannot see it on the shoulders of Sisyphus as he slowly climbs that hill? A burden or a promise: the humming wheel of rebirth as it engages in the circumambulation of our dreams. Can anyone enter into the pure

O-ness of things as it does? Exclamation, wonder, O is the loyal helpmate of exaltation. It dangles, like a bauble, dripping with silvery incandescence, a palpitating orb. Of all the letters, O partakes of never-ending form. Enclosure and limit are its chief acquisitions. It seeks out the mandala, the halo, and cosmic insignificance as a whorl of stars. We are all aware of its claim upon our being; it wants us to become immersed in the lost-ness of its imperious curve. Uroboros? Yes, that – and a sanctified image of vacancy orbiting itself.

... is the primary image of declension always reversing upon itself. Smooth like a snake it worms its way into our being, a letter of absolute renewal. No one knows its origin. On an ice-flow made blue by the demands of the sky, it becomes a vein of certainty meandering towards the sea. Oceans are amenable to its inversions: how often does it claw back the tide when the moon interposes? A royal letter, S abides in the scepter as regal desecration, a decree. What we learn from its prevarications is the adamancy of seeds as they assert their green shoots. S is indeed the Serpent, an ageless figure of fire, and the warmth of its embrace. We must be wary of its venom: one bite from this letter can inebriate the heart. S demands drunkenness from us, the final apotheosis of our spirit. Sibilance is its language; no letter slips from our mouths with such ease. In turn, we revere it as the perfect encisure on our bodies, a barely visible cicatrice. We venerate its perturbence, too, the sleek form of its writhing limbs.

... Oh, Templar disputation, a tidy blasphemy behind the walls of Jerusalem! This is a letter that causes havoc among those who conform. T scatters armies, shores up the act of retreat. It cuts a swathe through serried ranks. The hilt of a sword, it masquerade as martial art. Yet T possesses irony, too: Saint Francis made it into his pilgrim's staff whenever he set out on his Umbrian walks. A decapitated cross, by the Appian Way, it marked the end of rebellion when Spartacus was crucified. And on Christ's halo behind his felicitous head it reminds us of this shared event. T cohabits with crosstrees on chariots and the wishbone of camel saddles. Golf anyone, when the risible ball loops towards a distant hole? In a retort it bubbles, a supine figure of the Lapis. T becomes gold, the weighty periodicity of dense matter whose value transcends the miracle of every other element and the passage of a year. T is a gateway to light, the narrow aperture in a castle wall through which arrows fly to their target. Announce it to the world: T is the first meditation, the first Cross.

... is a bear ambling through a forest, cumbersome, hibernation firmly on its mind. Such a letter is a gathering of nuts before winter, one that prepares for dearth when snow smothers the ground. Those words that B supports bubble forth with dexterity because of its smooth and bulbous forms. The cheeks of our posterior, these are the supple forms of an athlete breasting the tape. "Be! and it is," so said the Logos, thus heralding in the full flush of time. This letter embodies both square and circle, the geometry of the orange mingled with the quadular base of a pyramid, a perfect resolution of the cosmos. B is like a dwarf star, drifting, drifting silently among wayward asteroids. No sound issues from is lips, as silence is its cohort. Hot air balloons bear it aloft like a basket, above the still earth at dawn. No one can disentangle B from the briar patch of thought. And yet it is a fulsome gift, myrrh set before a king in his rough stable. Contemplate its attachments: mother breasts that suckle at the beginning of the world. We are in awe of its deep assertions: in love does it enfold, white cloud above the horizon, a bird calling from the depth of a sacred grove.

... is leonine, thus said the Pharaoh. It finds its origin in hieroglyph and the ancient Greek lambda (Λ). L exercises an assimilating power over every consonant that it encounters, absorbing and amending as it abuts. Thus does it have the characteristics of an anemone and spawning coral. L is deeply palatal, its sound eerily suspended in the vault of a cathedral, plainsong among those angelic choirs. Or is it the tintinnabulation of a bell on feast days? We are confronted with a letter with OUM-like status, the most ancient possession of breath. Let us not hinder its aggregations, its solicitudes, as it rubs its fur against E and O like a cat. We are in the presence of a noble letter, one that secretly lies at the heart of the *Book of Kells*. Heed its ejaculations; they are the sound of breviary and the muted voice of psalms. No one knows where its voyage might end – in a coracle, perhaps, washed ashore on the shores of Icelandic sagas where words are the schema of power? Once it was known to have danced, trancelike, in Sufi tekkes where foot and leg are carefully choreographed. Such is the true nature of this letter: L, it seem, participates in the very act of prayer.

... is a canine letter, for it growls like a dog. Elevated to a battle standard, it routed an army outside the walls of Rome. A liquid letter of pure sound R stands before us, a pilgrim leaning on his staff. Or a tribesman perhaps, one foot on his knee and gazing into the distance, epiglottal noises of amazement on his lips. R saturates us with its sound, funnelling water down drainpipes as rain. An old Phoenician letter, much battered, it made Carthage its home. Therefore it has the Sahara in its veins, consanguine with aridity and absence. Of course it veils; the elect seek out disobedience as a mask to conceal the presence of true being in its form. R is thus a light deposited in the heart that is derived from the treasury of invisible realms. We must be heedful of its attributes: sometimes its opacity marks the beginning of altered states for us. R is vision's dream dreaming itself. No man can emerge from its maze unaltered. If Constantine made it his emblem at Malvien Bridge, this is because he perceived its mystical apparatus. R is the nearness of IT on a labarum surmounted by three golden orbs. It totters in the breeze. As a sign of victory such a letter lies at the heart of our need to conceal our not inconsequential deeds.

Oh epsilon, the first order of logic, maker of epithets and other disparate proofs! We are dealing here with connections and disjunctions. The cry of a gladiator when he jumped over lions in his chariot, its measure suggests 'many' from 'one', that old conundrum much debated in the Stoa. Indeed, philosophy is at its core. A man climbs up its laterals, seeking out invisible hierarchies. All who enter its precinct find themselves corralled. This is no stockyard, however, but a symptom of order. We stand within its bounds, limit our companion as we peruse the nature of its forms. Like all vowels, it escaped the net of the Etruscans when they composed their alphabet. They had no need for its sound as they marshalled their words. So it is a letter of absence par excellence! Like an octopus it conceals itself among plumes of ink on the sea floor. In consequence, all letters rely on a pen that is sharpened to the point of the Word. With the letter E we are in the hands of scribes. They sit in a square and compose missives for the lovelorn and the disenfranchised. Finally, we gaze at E as a hoopoe that flies high above Mount Qaf.

... is without peer when it comes to fashioning knots. A majuscule script on an illuminated manuscript, it loops and whorls with all the abandon of a carpet page in the *Lindisfarne Gospel*. On Skellig Michael, that rocky outcrop off Ireland, this letter stands on a promontory, bracing itself against Atlantic storms, a lonely figure of a monk. In K's presence, it seems, we are drawn into its life of asceticism and prayer. All who gaze upon it are reminded of the trepidation of ecstatic moments. Who but this letter can stand before us and deliver sermons? It's true, states of need are gift-laden carpets; they make up for any acts of fasting and all night vigils. K is a deep injunction to realize its true aspect, and to accept our lowliness in the wake of pride. Such a letter climbs Jebel Musa in Sinai, one step at a time. There before it is a vision of eternity unconstrained by mountain peaks and remote valleys. K is the voice of an anchorite sitting outside his cell: he feeds ravens words as they feed him bread, while any sign of passion is obliterated by the enormous silence of the dead. This letter stands before us as a principled god whose origin lies in a spring bubbling forth from Delphi's slopes. Castalia! Cleansing waters! No letter renews language more than K does. An incurable sweetness takes possession of the heart when it deigns to approach us.

Oh Q, Q, how delicate is your hue. Colour is your contagion, since you evoke all the tonalities of the desert. Your origin lies in the eye of a needle – or indeed in the gentle slope of a hill. No one know how you acquired such designations, but what we do know is that you travel in consort: the letter U is your constant companion. Is that hill of yours the primordial obelisk upon which a Phoenix lands each year after its long flight from Arabia? Has Q the substance of flame? Don't seek out permanency: in this letter the needle's eye is a gateway to those shifting formations of sand under our feet. Q is an armadillo bearing antique armour, knowing that the felicity of perfection is a part of its protective carapace. Or a stone axe, perhaps, is its designation, given that the prehistory of letters emerges from the mud just as salamanders do. Moreover, Q can be borne aloft like a warrior's shield! Heedful are we of its dichotomies, however: needle, sand, hillock and slope, all these pronounce verities that remain elusive. Q is thus the lasting configuration of mouth and tongue; it pouts when it approaches its beloved U. They lie together, in a palm grove, lovers forever in union.

... is a fugitive letter. It has no homeland, not Rome nor Carthage. Neither is it on the Cumae Tablet when Latin was first created. W came to be because of a fusion of two vagabond U's. It derives its strength from others. This is a thinking letter, able to adapt like a lizard. Books are seduced by its syllabilic utterance. In monastery scriptoriums it found its haven where the Great Questions were first given their voice. Once more W draws its strength from another letter in order to pronounce what we wish to know. When, Where, and Why, these questions orbit the H as it plods along a field of furrows. Nothing is fixed in the world of W: such a letter dances across the water like phosphorus in a ship's wake. We are dealing here with alteralities. When discarded, they induce detachment. W is constantly in league with beneficial knowledge whose rays of light expand in the mind, lifting a veil from the heart. There it stands, a stallion tethered outside a nomad's tent, preparing for flight. Bloodline is in its makeup. W harks back to a time when escutcheons on palace walls signaled a family's seigniorial inheritance. No harm comes to the soles of its feet when it ventures forth along this road.

What can one say about C? It's a letter of infinite curvature and grace that delicately floats above the line, uroboric and open. We are invited into its chamber. Crescent moon-shaped, C presides over the morning of our lives with all the resplendency and luminosity of fire. The tinder of this letter, however, is its own emptiness. No man can enter its space without encountering all the lassitude of absence. C is a place where bones are stored, the quiet haven of saints. Flesh and blood have been dispensed with in the interest of reconnoitering the sublime. Ossuaries are no place for the faint-hearted where such a letter finds its home. Is there light in this cave into which men are drawn? In there a man, long dead, kneels in prayer. He collapses into a pile of dust the moment one reaches out to grasp his hand. C is a letter of forbearance, the knowledge of Last Things. We are not opposed to its even-handedness: it dispenses with logic in a bid to determine the unfathomable. The lake at Shiz has the same depth. By water's edge a temple houses the Gusnasp fire, sacred to the elemental nature of C. Burn, then, in the cave of our hearts.

... is the first letter of manifestation. It transcends unity and polarity. The entire world comes into being through G as it ranges across the universe. Empowered by appearance it hangs as a mist above a lake, spreading diaphanously over the water, invoking a sense of levitation. Born of triunity, this letter wants to enter life as an engagement. Let us breathe in its airs. Like a medieval tapestry, G announces the Unicorn: unicity enhorned, the simple sanctity of a fabled beast allowed to graze in the fields of our mind. Thought is it herbage; no ruminant is thus permitted. What was once a camel's neck is now a more formal expenditure of energy. Gee! Where surprise emerges from its burrow like a platypus, scuppering the surface with its duck bill. Finally G enters the domain of solitary pools where spiders dance lightly over the surface. We are in the presence, it seems, of an old letter that has crossed the desert. It carries precious scrolls of holy writ and Akkadian tablets in the camel bags of royal emissaries. G is a travelling letter, a letter that reposes on a carpet when a caravan stops at night. There, among flickering flame and shadows, its inner heat melts down thought from ingots and recasts them at will.

... is the most upright of all the letters. World-tree, Yggdrasil, its origin lies in the depths of the forest. Who knows whether I's roots are buried in earth or in the air? Its verticality entices, and birds gather in its branches where they trill acorns as part of their confabulation. As a palm tree, I spreads its shadow on the ground with all the delicate tracery of fishnets. This is a god's letter, age-old Horus in the arms of his mother and her victory over Set. A giant fir on the island of Thule, I speaks to us as if out of the sun. A solar letter? No, that honour rests with H, in spite of its proximity to the moon. Gymnopedists understand I's language; they translate the language of the forest into coolness. Breath, wind among its leaves, we all know that is the spirit urging I to speak to us. A Dry Tree? Perhaps. Words, after all, are its fruit. The orange groves of Seville glow with the sweetness of its utterance. Unspoken is I's wood, and yet we aspire to hear its voice as sap coursing under bark. Taller than Babel, this letter's solitary stature makes it a target for tree fellers who loathe its perpendicularity. I is a letter of great spirit that towers over the world.

... is the most self-effacing of letters. It loses itself in the activity of others. In the words 'church' or 'thought' H becomes a mere sound. Or it escapes into such words as 'yacht' or 'naught'. Why is it so elusive? Does H prefer to be seen, not heard? But then, it suddenly turns up in the Greek letters 'chi' and 'rho', thus announcing the Redeemer to us all! H is like some Jurassic memory: the tooth of a dinosaur or the wing of some extinct bird. We are dealing here with evasion. H is therefore a very reclusive letter. It masquerades, it pretends. Not as some joker but as some inner light, for do we not know that it partakes of the sun? Could H be a mystical letter, one that suggest an alternate reality? Does it, in fact, keep company with angels? Or indeed... the god Hermes? This puts it in the proximity of the Primordial Alphabet, with Thoth himself. Again it merges with 'phi' to become 'f' as it refashions language! Let's admit it: H is no more than an exhalation of air as it rushes forth from the chest. 'Ha' becomes an excitation of spirit on one of its excursions from the body, a light that radiates. Clearly H must be an esoteric letter containing hidden information that means something else. At Stonehenge the Druids once worshipped it in the form of a prehistoric arch whenever the sun rose and set. Asceticism is in its bones: H spends its days among koans in a Zen temple, awaiting a slap across the shoulders by a master.

... is a conjunction between male and female, where the sun and moon are conjoined. It is the sign of cross-destinies whose centre is a small point. This is the point where pain and unity repose, and where ascension is intimated. Swordsmen fashion X's when they feint and parry, thereby alluding to the wound that pain engenders. We are in the presence of a magnificent letter that hovers like a palanquin over all. The destiny of X is prescribed: men die in its name, and martyrdom is part of its configuration. No man knows when he will be called upon to take up his own X and begin his march towards Golgotha. Doves hover above his head, telling him that he is once more in the care of some supernatural energy, a puissance given to but few men. X is none other than the letter of apotheosis, a moment of heaven-ward engagement. Transfiguration is X's greatest asset, we are told. No one knows when (and if) he might be called to its place of revelation. Sails on ships are filled with its gusts when a voyage towards wind-roses is assured. X, indeed, is a sign of transcendence, the still point at the centre of the world. We are forever in its thrall.

... is clearly the First Question, the why and wherefore of existence. Such a letter plunges us into the abyss. Found among runes, it also surfaces in Arabic as the vowel *waw*, the first letter of ibseity. A truly cosmic letter, Y represents the absoluteness of non- manifestation. It rests in silence. In that silence it pursues the secret transcendence of the world. No letters stands above it save that of A, which possesses the secret of the secret of Y. In this consonant, therefore, we have entered into the realm of pure metaphysics. Other letters stand before us, their pennants fluttering before us on the field of ethereality and grace. Such a noble army! In contrast, Y is a cool letter without peer: unlike those others, which thrive on humidity and dryness, it has no geometry other than that of the sphere. If it is true that trees war among themselves, and that Y as a yew tree remains aloof, this is because such a consonant is a loner. Its gnarled contortions seal Y's reputation as an oracle. It sees and perceives. No man can utter it without questioning himself. Wherever we go, however we think, the Y of things continues to invest in inquiry. Now we know what constitutes the abyss of this letter: like an old tribesman Y stands on a bluff, gazing into the unutterable reaches of memory. It sees what we do not see.

... is a deep well of renewal. The water jar is its anchor to the world. Under a dolmen it marks the very womb of the earth. We gather by its rim to talk and to share a common ease. U's origin lies in the floodplains of Egypt where men gathered to celebrate the Festival of the Waters. Black soil, alchemy, the transmutation of base metal into gold. Nor does it ever stray far from Q, the divine vulva, birth-canal of gods. When a word is shipwrecked, it is U that rights its splintered masts. In such a letter dwell a congregation of sages. When they speak, their words glow like embers. It is true: letters keep us alive; when we die it is always the result of a frustrated word. Because of its abundance U never transgresses the limits of language. U is both fecund and outreaching: it flows forth as enlivening waters, veritas in a cup. We honour its fluidity. Up-blaze of fountains! This is U's quest: all clarities are contained in its bowl. Therefore we must consider U as a perfect receptacle. We carry it on our shoulders, down cobbled lanes, water inside glistening as sunlight, its contents forever intimating the aqueous nature of heaven.

... is a warrior's axe, or the paddle on a Tahitian war canoe.
Both brandish power and strength with aplomb, because P
is an instrument of aggression linked to ancient etiquette.
This letter is bulging with muscle. Long limbs on a discus
thrower are replete with its physical dexterity. P forges
division by cutting things in half, making such severance
an act of defiance! Yet there is ambivalence in this letter.
Its martial clamour is softened by labial pronouncement.
P escape through the lips, we know, as a gentle breath.
Moreover, as a vocable it suggests a solitary adventure
across the frontiers of utterance. Among ruins it wanders,
searching for ostraca that records a genuine inner movement
of the mind. Thinking is one of P's greatest attributes; it is
in thought that this letter truly resides, a gnomic utterance
pithy with a philosopher's diatribes. P is a letter that hangs
out in the Stoa, looking for insights. We, too, find ourselves
enmeshed in its ganglion of questions. These are designed
to enliven, whereas answers kill. Let us, then, place it on
a plinth outside a temple. It stands there like an animal-
headed god, a reed in hand. Finally, it seems, P is the lasting
blossom of concord masquerading as petals.

... is a lonely letter. It has no known origin, and is spurned by the Cumae Tablet. Where does one begin to enunciate its persona? As a fishhook perhaps, jagging on a clump of coral? Our mind is free to wander to those words that make it their own. Justice, jazz, and the small rodent known as a jerboa, for example. Or in the Arab word, *judhb*, which causes us to think of celestial attraction and supernatural blessings. Oh yes, it also appears in the Great Snake, Jarapiri, said to have created the world. So J partakes of the mesmerizing effect of *creatio ex nihilo*. Now we are plunging deep into the maelstrom of causelessness, where nothing becomes a double negative. J revels in this conundrum: it means that it can be and not be at the same time. This puts it in the company of Plato, who dealt in such absurdities with relish. A letter without etymology? Hardly, since he who boasts a scimitar in his belt is protected by the power of J. Fire-wielder, prepare to dazzle us with flames! Does it not resemble a shepherd's crook or a round-bale hook? Let us give it our blessing as a working tool. And then watch: J stalks along forest trails, solitary, opportunistic, partial to water, its spots blending in with leaves and mottled shadow.

Why does the letter D not remonstrate with its boldness? Is it because it finds itself incomplete, a hemisphere and not a circle? The Greeks made D into a triangle in their bid to give it a more definite geometric form. They wanted it to reflect a groundedness and the glimpse of a high summit. D is therefore a chameleon switching from one form to another. In the Jewish letter, Daleth, it represents the Names of God. If D reflect these Names, does it mean that the letter is a veil? Or rather, if the language of God is the language of absence, could D be a substitute for the Word? This consonant does indeed preface the word Deus, thus ensuring its perfection in the wake of nomenclature. So many names! Can the world do without them when nature itself remains mute? D is thus a hand reaching out for our attention: it wants us to recognize the aspirations of our inner life, in spite of the troubles that we might encounter. In this sense D is a parting of the veil. It allows us to enter ourselves. Clearly D is a letter that brings comfort and brief moments of wellbeing. We should raise it to the top of a mast, a fluttering pennant that signals victory and homecoming.

... is the letter denoting Universal Man. It is the principle of unity and its manifestation. This is a letter of deep import for the future of humanity. Buried in its depths is a sense of humankind's spiritual evolution. As V is invoked in our thoughts, so too is our believe in the possibility that consciousness is not fixed. V urges us to think beyond our am-ness. It's no accident that the word 'universe' alerts us to the unicity of poetry, for 'verse' is a part of its substance. Universal Man is thus a poem in himself. In formation V becomes a companion to cranes when they fly south. It is a letter of the sky, always elevated, a sign of victory when all seems lost. Could it be, too, that vagrancy and vagabondage are a part of its nature? A true gyrovague it wanders from monastery to monastery, an emissary of language eager to embrace much that the world offers. Things are identified and given substance through words, and V herds them across the plains of anonymity, its whip tracing arcs of sound in the air. Vigor and wandering are its signs. Universal Man calls no place his home, nor does V, and yet is ever at our side. We are beholden to its aerial peregrinations.

The origin of the letter F lies in the early Semitic alphabet – in the letter *'waw'*. Waw is the letter of cosmic expression and, like V, is aligned to the concept of Universal Man. It is a cold letter and thus bestows a certain slowness on how we create a word. Its antiquity suggests a chick or a mace, and one sees its image in the Greek letter 'phi' (Φ). As rudimentary as it is, one could also imagine it as an old carding-comb removing burrs from a Golden Fleece. Flecks of gold tantalise us with their absence. We are in the hands of a letter that arranges and separates. Wisdom is its object. It wants to eliminate cant from our vocabulary. In this sense F is an iconoclast. It is one of those letters that moves from place to place, tearing down shibboleths in its bid to cleanse the way we think. Moreover, as a mace it breaks things apart. Though not a storm trooper, F nonetheless impresses us with its martial vigour. It stands on the edge of *apeiria*, the unlimited, wishing us to define our own limits. F represents the unqualified good in ourselves. When we heed its message, our own Golden Fleece glitters anew with flecks of gold. The fire of contradiction thus delivers us into a new life at the behest of such a letter.

... is the sign for water and, like water, represents the highest good. It gives life to ten thousand things and never strives. Indeed, it flows into places that most men reject. It also retains allegiance to the Hanged Man in the Tarot pack, and so represents self- sacrifice. The gallows on which the Hanged Man hangs upside down is none other than the Tree of Knowledge. Thus M stands for martyrdom, prudence, and the creation of humankind as the Great Work. We are thus in the presence of a letter with alchemical connotations. Does it partake of the Philosopher's Stone? Does it seek to transform us through its quintessential nature? These are questions that go to the heart of M's reserve. It is a secretive letter. It thrives on the fluidity of its essence. In a retort it bubbles mysteriously, a concoction that suggests an elixir, a draught perhaps made from the white-flowered moli, a magical herb. To drink of M is to enter into a state of salubrity. There one becomes the Hanged Man seeking after knowledge. There one hangs upside down bedevilled by a look of bliss. Entrancement is the result of this act, not suffering. Haloes might become us, even though we would prefer to dismiss them as so much clutter. M challenges us to reverse our stance: head down, the earth is even closer to our thoughts. With this letter at our side protecting us, we are ready to embark upon the Great Work ourselves.

... is a double-axe bound together in reverse, a rattlesnake poised to strike. Cultic perhaps, symbol of the labyrinth? Zeus lurks in its blind alleys, the god of thunder, therefore supreme among those who lived on Mount Olympus. It's hard to know whether this letter is malevolent or awesome. Placed at the end of the alphabet, Z suggests the emergence of Last Things as a pivot to existence. We cannot escape its finality, its desire to remind us of the contingent nature of being. We die at its behest; and yet we live because it posits renewal as a prospect. Who among us has the courage to strike back? Z rears up and spatters us with its poison. Yet this poison is not death-dealing but wisdom, the wise snake encoiled. On the walls of Knossos we see its image transformed into a butterfly! Snake, labyrinth, double-axe and Minoan goddess, all these images reside in its depth. Z is thus a fraternal letter, a letter that embodies truths that cannot be uttered. It relies on its own menagerie of symbols to convey what can never be said. A letter of pure artifice, a sharp blade married to a snake's clear-eyed gaze, Z is thus a primal energy that enlarges our capacity to be. Its home is the Underworld where it presides over the fashioning of myths.

... is the final letter on our journey through the alphabet. And yet it is the first, the Alpha of all letters. A is an ox's head with its horns upended, a vowel of unity and universal polarity. As a white island it marks the centre of the world, the primordial egg. Some see it as the true Orient of Lights, and the first upright letter associated with Adam. All letters emerge from its bountiful harvest. It is in every letter, and so embodies the act of transmutation. Without A, the alphabet would crumble into dust. Only the Word would exist then, the Logos that utters the cosmos. Silence would forever reign as a disembodied vowel. Is it also a divining rod seeking out water? Yes, in that it aligns itself with M's fluidity in presenting being to ourselves in the form of I AM. When the ego is tossed to one side, however, Being is freed to hover above us like an eagle. We gaze into its enormous glory. We see the endlessness of its penetrations. A is thus a ladder, a gauntlet, a fakir's rope ascending into the sky. Whether we climb or push past it A challenges us with its penchant for otherness. The letter of all letters, it haunts us with its primacy. When we bow before A's rung and its apex, then do we experience apotheosis. It is the key to our inner life, that locked room where selfhood is imprisoned. To open that room, finally, is to allow letters under the authority of A to come forth in their bid to name everything that exists. Before them A will be conducted in stately fashion under a palanquin, an unexampled grace, regal and yet simple in its ornamentation and dress.

REFLECTIONS

I must be true to the alphabet. It is the perfect discursus of my dreams. When I begin to fall asleep at night I see letters spiraling to earth like leaves. They are writing to me. They are telling me that I must hold onto their delicate perambulations. G, R, M, for example, lie there in dappled light. When I add three vowels, O, E, and E to these, a word begins to emerge in my thoughts. 'Goreme'. A place of tufa chapels in Central Turkey, among rock monasteries. Long ago I travelled there as a young writer. I wanted to place myself among those ancient frescoes and carved columns, to feel their antique power. Here began my journey into the world of Byzantium. Here I gained my first glimpse of the Word.

~

In a monastery on Mount Athos I attended my first liturgy. Greek words flowed from the mouths of monks sitting in stalls fervently fingering their prayer knots with gnarled hands. Their chanting captivated me. I felt myself participating in a colloquium of sound emanating from a high place. The quiet ecstasy of monks. They bore words within their breasts with all the humility of those prayer knots. Each knot, I realized, was a call to enter into the spirit of the Word. I had come to a place where a celestial language was still spoken.

~

How can one not embrace the majesty of the word? It is like a carpet woven by serried hands. I can see the shuttle speeding back and forth across the loom. This is my gesture towards the evolution of forms through language. I am weaving magic, the concatenation of beauty and of images. My language is one of gemstones on a scabbard: they glow with hidden menace.

~

Prayer is my secret amanuenses. I listen to its directives. Theophanic words tumble from the lips of saints, men of silence and of the Word. I have met them in their desert caves, on forest paths between hermitages, in temple corridors among rock gardens. I have heard their words of welcome uttered in numerous languages – Greek, Italian, Coptic, Arabic, Spanish, Hindu, and Japanese. All words are the same. Fraternity is a verb as well as a noun.

~

All my life I have lived among words, from my first library book to the cryptic carvings of myths on bamboo wafers tied together by a Balinese priest. Words have long congregated in the corridors of my mind. Adventitious text, the promulgation of stories as the first step towards understanding. When an old Aboriginal[1] tribesman permitted me to touch the carvings on his tjuringa

1 A tjuringa is a sacred stone that depicts Dreaming events. They are used to conjure up such events at times of ritual. They have no origin except as timeless artifacts. They are passed down from one custodian to the next, thus insuring that the sacred stories, these celestial letters, remain alive to the generations.

stone inside a sacred cave, I knew then that words partook of symbols whose context was revelation.

~

Interiorizing words, they have become as corpuscles in my blood. They enliven, they transmit energy to the far reaches of my body. Words are made flesh; they enclose my body in the subtle nuance of meaning. I begin to mean something to myself.

~

The heart is a repository of words, of suffering, anguish, and uncertainty. We bleed when certain words are uttered. I hear them pumping through my veins, the dark blood of despair mingle with hope.

~

Even as death approaches, the drums on outer islands replicate the sounds of the earth. They are calling to me, these skin-covered hollowed out logs shaped like charging horns, urging me to heed their voices. Tympanums reverberate with hand-induced songs. They are calling to me from across the waters.

~

Where will I be yesterday? The future tense grappling with the past. Who am I tomorrow? Again this tinkering with the ever-shifting nature of persona in the region of muddled time. I am nobody. I am a conglomeration of actions masquerading as words.

~

I note that each letter in the alphabet contains what medieval French scribes used to call in their Book of Hours an ystoire. *In their careful calligraphic work, bound to desk and parchment as they were, these men used to historiate individual letters and give them visual life. Thus each ystoire becomes an 'illumination' filled with immaculate colour, the colour of inner knowledge. I therefore try to make my letters depict a verbal ystoire in the same way. It is no accident that in the opening verses of a Book of Hours the letter D contains the portrait of an angel or a face. When the words* Domine labia mia aperies... *('O Lord open my lips...') come forth from the letter D in the opening verse of such a book, it heralds the advent of the Word. We are at once alerted to the link between image and utterance. These are the images of adjudication and of grace.*

~

Nor is it an accident that the goddess Pallas Athena is often portrayed gazing down at a boundary stone, that battered herm by the wayside, while applying a finger to her forehead. Hermes is the god of writing, after all, and so an intermediary between the inchoate energies of the earth and those of the intellect. Words are thus tiny phantasms of the mind, a god on the border between the real and the imagined. I note that the ancients called her 'Tristona' because of her three-fold capacity for apprehension - that of the intellectible, the intelligible, and the natural. Her daemon haunted Olympus as the eloquence of the word. No wonder she and Hermes saw eye to eye.

~

It is said that men once saw the physical world with the eye of the flesh, and with the eye of reason they saw themselves. And thirdly, with the eye of contemplation they saw within themselves. It begs a question, however: is self-knowledge the product of our eye in league with words? It is only with these that we are able to contemplate what we least know about ourselves.

~

I read in one of Hugh of Saint Victor's works a discussion about the 'perfection' of letters. Letters, he said, are found in every discourse, for the very sounds they make are letters. All wisdom is thus compressed into a nugget of thought when words act gently upon themselves. Words are never abrasive, he tells us, when they respect the integrity of one another.

~

The word 'mystery' I am told is derived from the Greek word 'mu', indicating a 'closed mouth'. Does this mean that words should not be uttered if mystery is to be assured? And yet, silence also speaks. It may be that words surrender to the power of silence when self-revelation is upon us.

~

Some words lie on the ground like spent cartridges after a gun fight. Nepsis, theosis, apodixis, what do they mean to us today? The sensibility lodged in such grave utterance is lost to us. All of these words, clearly, are of Greek origin. It suggests to me that such words were known around the Stoa by men who were familiar with a thinking that was utterly free from the tangible. Unlike planet in their orbits, these men had developed a trajectory of their own that was entirely otherworldly. They thought in a way that allowed them to exist in an interplanetary capacity. Space, for them, was the nexus between words.

~

Back to my alphabet. I think of some words and compliment them on their blandness. Take the word 'unit' for example, and view what seems to be its unexampled clarity. It may pertain to number or to a cupboard of some sort. Should I dismiss it as unworthy of my time? Yet, if I take the trouble to re-arrange its letters, I come up with a French word, nuit. Ah, so the night has at last emerged from its darkness, a word that embraces 'tenebrous'. What a beautiful word. It means dark, shadowy, or obscure. I am now of the opinion that 'unit' lives multiple lives in the shade of itself. It encloses, it conceals. When letters and words interpose a frisson results.

~

Recovery is an important word that I associate with words. When we know a word intimately, we recover its true meaning. Etymology is the science of recovery in this respect. When a word's origin is unveiled I feel that I am embracing an absolute.

99

Letters are but fragments of this absolute, scintillas perhaps of Al Tirmidhi's ethereal 'lights'. We must, therefore, remember that words possess an etymological life. The debris of past thinking lies in their 'tenebrous' striations.

~

I keep thinking of the medieval monk Tuotilo whom I encountered in the monastery of St. Gallen in Switzerland. He designed and carved in ivory and precious gems a beautiful Evangelium Longum, or Gospel, for Charlemagne. I keep asking myself why a book, however elaborate it might be, should become the object of a king's desire. Words on vellum have a specific density, it seems. Was Tuotilo aware of his power to entrance? His deft fingers, knives, and nibs had created a remarkable statement, however: the life of the Word wrapped in the ivory of words. No wonder Charlemagne set himself the task of learning how to read and write.

~

At the time of King Alphonso X of Toledo, men gathered from all over Europe to translate Arabic texts into Latin. Men such as Gerard of Cremona and John of Seville sat down with Jew and Moorish linguists to render books originally written in ancient Greek. Thus the works of Aristotle, Plato, Galen, and Hippocrates were provided with new clothes stitched together from the cloth of Latin. Words travelled along trade-routes of the mind through Cairo, Kairouan, and Cordova to be translated anew for scholars in the cathedral schools of Chartres, Paris, and Oxford.

This was a time when men were hungry for fresh ideas. Quills, inks, parchment and erasers were pressed into service at the School of Translators in Toledo. Words were fashioned with patience and care by scribes eager to shed new light on knowledge. Such a caravan of the intellect, ship's cabins and camel bags bulging with thought from distant lands! It is hard to imagine the excitement these translators experienced when a copy of Ptolemy's Almagest *or* Euclid's Elements of Geometry *were laid before them on their desks. A new book had arrived!*

It is at this point that I begin to ask myself about the true nature of such a Kingdom of Letters, words newly realized by the alphabet of the wise. Can a man not shed his wonder at such a remarkable trade in thoughts and ideas? I try to position myself at the elbow of Gundisalvi as he begins to shape a fresh quill. He, like others nearby, is about to serve the word. Letters are his tools. And while he fashions sentences on parchment the whole of Europe attends. The miracle of Greek philosophy is about to blossom once more.

This is a story that will not leave me. I have journeyed to Toledo, to Kairouan, Cairo, Fez and Cordova, to Paris and Chartres in pursuit of this elusive chimera or words. The world is a better place because of their wanderings, I tell myself. We hear them coming, across space and time, stowed in a merchant's baggage or sea-chest along with bolts of damask and precious oils. I am in the company of logosthetes wearing fine silks and turbans.

Truly, the alphabet has been well served. All its letters are replete with the prospect of reviving Greek philosophy into another language. Latin is richer for it, and scriptoriums across Europe are aflame with its gifts. Once more thought is carefully crafted into uncial and majuscule letters on the parchment of the mind.

~

I see myself as a goose quill about to plunge into a pot of ink. Words drip from my thoughts.

~

Whenever I gaze at a photograph in my study depicting a bookseller from Cairo, seated in his tiny booth in the old part of town, while reading from an open folio cross-legged, I think of a painting that I also possess of a scribe in the square of Marrakech writing down a billet doux for a young woman. Both images come from a far place, where words are treasured. Love and the book are intertwined. Only a butterfly would understand how I feel: its wings open and close like a book whenever it lands on a bush. Words are on its wings, and the trace of proteins from its *hardened scales soaks up energy from the sun. For that old man in Cairo, too, the book in his hands is a ray of sunlight.*

~

Old books gravitate towards me with the alacrity of rolling stones. I possess twelve small volumes of Homer's epics that I discovered in a second-hand bookshop in Buenos Aires, published in 1787. A friend in Zurich presented me with the Complete Works of Lord Byron in a First Edition. A third volume, printed in Madrid in 1588, is a Book of Devotions that another friend in Barcelona offered to me as a memento. Two of these works are in foreign languages. When I read them they speak to me from the depths of their unfamiliarity. Suddenly I begin to realize why: there is resonance in a diction not your own. In that moment the alphabet grows wings and flies high up into the branches of some exotic tree. This is the nature of old books, especially those in other languages: they perch above us like peacocks, their tails intimating a lingual beauty made up of inestimable colours.

I think of libraries where books are stabled like race horses. They range across endless tiers of shelves in leather volumes while I mentally caress their spines. In St. Catherine's monastery below Mount Sinai I was granted an audience with an early copy of The Triads *by Gregory Palamas. In the library of Abbey of St Gallen I first set eyes on Tuotilo's* Evangelium longum *in its ivory cover, as well as the mummy Schepenese in her coffin.[2] Libraries are the equivalent of space probes; they enter the unlimited universe of knowledge and relay it back to earth. Borges likened the universe to a library too, so I am in good company. In contrast, Letizia Alvarez of Toledo, his playful pseudonym, observed that a vast library is useless. She suggested that a single volume would be sufficient to house all knowledge. If this were so, where would I go then to sate my passion for words?*

~

....

[3] This mummy was the subject of a chapter in *A Mapmaker's Dream.*

I begin to ask myself as to whether letters actually communicate. When they are alone they barely speak to one another. But when they enter a word they at once make sense of things. Inertia gives way to empathy.

~

All five stars of the Southern Cross have adopted Greek letters as their names, it seems. It is no wonder that they glimmer with pertinence.

~

On the ancient Roman Cumae Tablet a triangle of three large circles enclose a smaller one. Around these outer circles the Latin alphabet wends its way like a column of ants. Are these circles cogs depicting a verbal machine, a calendric mechanism? No, they are not tinkering with time but with the eternal matrix between image and expression.

~

Buried words recovered from their graves in remote villages along the Nile. The Rosetta Stone in three languages, hieroglyphic, demotic, and Greek, tells us of the glory of gods and the beneficence of a Pharaoh. At Nag Hammadi, too, the Gnostic Gospels were unearthed by a farmer in his field. Champollion, along with modern scholars, spent half a lifetime translating for us to read. Each is a compendium of hieratic verses that commemorate the extraordinary. God speak through these old languages. Encrusted in dirt, their letters yet announce the indelible nature of utterance. No famine or flood can drown the lasting effects of language upon our thoughts. When the gods speak, words attain to their true station.

~

There is an ancient tradition that links Palamedes, one of Homer's heroes, to the invention of Greek letters. He, along with the three Fates, are accredited with seventeen of these letters. Another

107

suggestion is that Thoth took his inspiration from cranes flying in the sky to render vowels. These birds, apparently, brought them from Egypt to Greece where they were finally offered to the Etruscans, who adapted them into the Latin alphabet.

I am intrigued by these associations. Fates, birds, and Trojan heroes, all had their part to play creating the alphabet. This is a heady mix. I am beginning to suspect that letters are by nature migratory; they enjoy moving from place to place. Is this not the essence or language? Each word is a migration of thought from a lonely place of muteness to those sumptuous halls of knowledge.

The question is: are letters but feathers that intimate flight?

~

Let me confess: I am consumed by letters. A logomaniac, perhaps? Possibly. They swarm through my mind as do disciplined squads of soldier crabs on a mud flat. This is how language works. It is less a force of nature than one of intellect. When we accept words into our lives, we are the servants of consciousness. Life may be a fissure of uncertainty, a rocky headland of anxiety, but with words we are able to smooth the waters.

Am I a prisoner of Babel? All these languages, all these letters manning the battlements. They are there to repulse the hoards. I stand on the rampart, my pen a crossbow aimed into the void. No one knows better than I what awaits me if I miss the mark.

~

When we fashion our first letters with sloping line-guides under the page, it is a moment when they fix themselves in our minds forever. As motherhood imprints itself on a child, so do letters imprint themselves on our psyches. Then do we begin to flow through life as a sentence. Leaning a language is to be initiated into the secrets of our culture. Tribal people formalize their right of passage so that they might articulate their world as myth. Wolf children never know such an experience, and remain mute when removed from the wild. In contrast, language is the diadem with which we crown our lives. To be human is announced when we utter our first word.

~

Language is not the same as letters. Pre-literate societies possess language, and are able to express their thoughts with words. They are then able to articulate their myths, their lore, and their songs through the use of language, and with the aid of memory. It is only when the alphabet comes into play that memory is eclipsed.

A man re-minds himself of his origin through language. With letters he records his memories. The difference between the two lies in the act of externalization. Writing is an act of externalization. Letters turn inwardness into a process of externalization.

Some might argue that consciousness is refined by the process of writing. More subtle permutations are thus addressed. The tragedy of the wolf-child is that he cannot think in words. He can only think by way of impressions. His world is entirely dependent upon the use of his senses.

The transformation of ours senses into words is made complete through the alchemy of letters. Language is therefore the final realization of thought. Our senses still continue to play their part, of course, but now they are modified by words. And words, for a pre-literate society, have yet to attain to the reality of signs.

It is through the genius of letters that this is made possible. Letters bestow upon cognition a physical dimension. They make tangible the act of thinking. We do not think in words as such, until we actually write down our thoughts.

Letters are the primary tools for articulating thought. They are the retort in which we distill our impressions.

~

If Thoth found his inspiration for the creation of letters in the flight of cranes, why did he not encourage his people to abandon hieroglyphs? I suspect because he could not give up his love of images, and so was content to allow his letters to fly to Greece. The question must then be asked: what do clouds represent? Punctuation?

~

His beak is like a stylus, his ink the black earth of the Nile floodplains. As an ibis Thoth wanders along levee banks, looking for letters. But no, he prefers hieroglyphs because they depict images, not letters. In his eyes the palpable still reigns over the abstract, as Chinese characters also attest.

~

What does it mean to be a servant of words? Except to say that their arrangement on paper is as substantial as any electrical impulse. A finely crafted sentence has the power to light up the mind. It shines a beam into our cerebrum that is as sharply defined as that of any laser. Words, too, ripple across the mind with all the vivacity of quicksilver in a Moorish fountain. They shimmer, they pulsate.

~

There is a long history of libraries being burnt to the ground in the interest of orthodoxy, whether religious or secular. Ibn Masarra, we know, was ordered to burn his writings because they were perceived to be heretical, just as Peter Abelard was forced to publicly burn his book Theologia *in Soissons for the same reason. Abd-ar-Rahman's library was destroyed by his son 'Al-Hakim II because it housed too many books on science. The library of the Sarapeum in Alexandria, too, met its end at the hands of a Christian mob in the fourth-century. As late as the*

21st century libraries in Iraq and Sarajevo have been condemned to the flames. The implication, of course, is that words can be incendiary. They must be reduced to ashes so that thought might be contained. Words, it seems, are the tinder of our minds, and are therefore dangerous.

~

Are libraries so dangerous? Klein, in Elias Canetti's novel, Auto da Fe, seems to think so. He attempts to take letters prisoner, to free himself from their contagion. Yet still they beat him to a pulp. In the end, he is buried under a cascade of books whose letters kick him until he is almost senseless.

Is this the revenge of the book? I cannot believe it. It might be the revenge of a library that has been misused, abused, not seen as Borges tells us – as an endless mystique of corridors leading everywhere and nowhere. Libraries are all we possess to bolster us against the relentless intrusion of facts into our lives.

~

The Chinese possess a symbolic system of letters known as Wen. Such a system has no echo among the ordinary language of daily intercourse. Wen has the capacity to express everything, yet draws its function exclusively from the position it occupies on the page. The meaning that Wen articulates depends solely on the fact that it is there and not there at one and the same time. Connected by laws as limpid as the thought of the ancients, and as simple as the musicality of numbers, each letter is suffused with intelligence. Yet equally, they disdain to be read. They do not express, they signify.

It is said that these Wen ideograms tolerate neither ignorance nor clumsiness. Their script is truly beautiful. When a wealthy man was buried in China, his coffin was suspended over a stele adorned with Wen letters recording his virtues and responsibilities in life. Chinese Wen characters were thus a prelude to the man's entry into heaven. Words and letters preceded him as a celestial language that enhanced his reputation in the eyes of his ancestors.

I am beginning to sense something mortuary about letters. They bury us in the wisdom known only to a flight of cranes.

~

I begin to see how important letters are to the conduct of celestial thought. Like the Chinese, Aborigines also speak such a language when they engage in secret rites. Words, so ordained, protect the unwary from the power of heavenly engagement. They therefore act as a shield as much as a weapon.

~

Let us not pretend: Letters are the brocade we use to decorate our thoughts.

~

The Romans, I believe, were the first European nation to decorate their monuments with honorifics. Even the Greeks shied away from such verbal extravagance. Which suggests that their was a guild of scribes in stone who lived in the vicinity of quarries. With chisel and mallet they patiently carved out words to resist the erosion of time. Letters were used to announce immortality. In such a way, it seems, the alphabet became the bedrock of our immortal worth.

~

In Borneo, among the Iban people, I encountered their script as a series of markings on bamboo wafers. These, I was told by story custodians, had replaced an earlier, more elaborate form of writing suggestive of Chinese ideograms. The latter were so badly smudged by floodwaters that caused all memory of their existence to be lost. The Iban were forced to use a substitute script to help them fashion their stories.

The idea that an alphabet might be lost to us, and a new one fashioned to replace it, struck me as a precarious event. I can imagine the Iban people feeling a deep nostalgia for their lost letters, their ideograms, washed away by a flood. The blurring of words seems to me to be an important issue. Where do we go to find the truth of ancient edicts once more? At a time when our own languages and forms of expression have become so emasculated by digital interference merely highlights how the alphabet has become the servant of abbreviation. In the interest of verbal succinctness we want our words to lose their sovereignty as true integers of thought.

The Iban people understood this crisis as they struggled to re-invent their alphabet. What they restored was wafer-thin, its slenderness a testament to the fragility of language itself. All they possess now are rudimentary markings, the final desecration of the immutable, tor-like structure that was once their letters.

~

Herodotus, I note, suggested that the Garamantians, a remote kingdom in Libya, screeched like bats when they spoke. How often do we hear an unfamiliar language and come to the same conclusion? Words in league with nature's voice is not something we feel comfortable with. And yet, I now believe that language is a fulsome excrescence of nature, its way of allowing us to interpret what it has to say.

~

We rarely push words beyond the limit of what they mean. Even as metaphors we are happy to see them in the context of age-old clichés. Hot/hell, white/snow, heavy/lead, such metaphors satisfy what we expect of them. Homer's metaphors may strike us as fresh, those such as 'wine-dark sea' or 'grey-eyed goddess', but to their listeners they were as conventional to the ear as ours. Yet it is only when we break with such conventions that true poetry begins to savor of something pure. Then words begin to sing anew.

~

I have tried to release letters from the prison of their neutrality as sounds only, in order to allow them to attain to a more vertical dimension as signs. It is there that the realm of metaphysics comes into play. Like seaweed they drift across our interior vision, absorbed in their amorphous arrangements, reaching out to entangle us in what is often indescribable. We long for them to realize new shapes.

~

Letters, and therefore words, are the mediatrix between the real and the contingent. They span the world between pretext and context. Without letters – that is, before the advent of writing – humankind relied on the spoken word through the aegis of metaphor and ritual. Letters as sounds thus imposed a numinosity upon the spoken word that invoked a new dimension to thought and expression. The word 'hagiography' denoted this new dimension when it finally realized itself as text. It means "holy script", which placed the activities of certain men and women at centre-stage. They became not just heroes as in a recited epic (Homer), but as transcribers of the real. They had become scriptural. Saints and sages were thus 'written down', their actions becoming the summit of the interior life.

~

Our word 'metaphor' means 'to carry from beyond'. That is, to bring into being a portion of the real so that it might appear, for a time, contingent. The lives of great sages and prophets are metaphors (hagiography). They make knowledge of the numinous to which we might begin to identify. Men such as Buddha, Socrates, Christ, and Antony of Egypt acted out the real. They did not write it down as text because they regarded words on paper as a limit.

~

In one of his more profound statements, made to his friends at dinner a few days before his death, Christ informed them that he no longer wished to speak to them in parables (John 16:23). The time for analogy and comparison was over, and plain speech had become the order of the day. Like Socrates, he wanted his words to settle upon his friends with all the succinctness of a non-narrative. It was at this point that his speech travelled beyond metaphor and entered the domain of the connatural. That is, into the essence of nature. He finally revealed himself as the Word. Nothing quite like it had ever happened before in the history of language: a man had become the Word and finally entered into the sanctity of language itself.

~

The alphabet is our primary tool of speculative thought. Without letters we would have no way of recording how we think. It is no accident that those early Arab philosophers formulated a system of letters to aid them in their metaphysical investigations. They knew that only through the use of letters could they fashion words. Speculative linguistics enabled them to break with the placidity of conventional thought, which they believed ill-served the growth of their inner reality.

The metaphysics of language enabled them to bridge the gap between physis and pneuma, between physical reality and the spiritual. Letters were not only bird-given, but of the very essence of thoughtful endeavor. We think in words and so open up pathways towards a more profound state of spiritual insight. Albert Einstein knew this to be true when he finally resorted to letters in order to devise his theory of relativity. E =MC could not have been realized without the aid of letters. Ludwig Wittgenstein also resorted to letters to argue his case for what he called truth-grounds.

Without words, whether verbal or written, we could never have envisioned the universe. Stars and planets are thus cosmic words; they articulate universal order. Galileo and Kepler, for example, explored the heavens for the sole purpose of expressing infinity. For their part letters silenced the mythic mind, and so introduced us to the pure metaphysics of the word.

The alphabet is a neurological miracle. It has allowed us to plumb the depths of ourselves. The entire cosmos does not exist save as an extension to the word. Letters, therefore, represent the quiddity of being. Their essence is both neurological and cosmological. When we think we draw upon the stars in order to shape our universe. More than numbers, which are the primary integers of order only, letters offer us the fluidity of speculation so that we might understand the role of being in Being.

~

The god of letters is a 'noetic light'. When he bestows his radiance upon us we glow like the sun. No temple can contain him because he inhabits the temple of our minds. The alphabet is an instrument of prognostication, a prophesy of the sublime.

~

We stand before the alphabet as a supplicant. It bestows on us the fullness of being. We do not exist outside its composite of letters. They enfold us in manifold aspects of Primary Being like the wings of a Cherubim, aflame with the numinosity of the cosmos as an infinite source.

~

Letters dispense with polarities. One and two may make three, we know, the first truinity of existence. Number sets up quantity and extension, no more. All twenty-six letters, however, offer us their orchestra of sounds, each as subtle as finger cymbals on the hands of a Balinese dancer. It is these sounds that we hear when we pronounce A, B, C, D etc. They constitute the most humble prayer of speech.

~

The Book of Letters *utterly consumes me. It has become a mystical proposition that I am unable to bear.*

~

In the word 'lover' the French word 'voler' is buried, meaning 'to fly'. In this way, letters offer us a road to transcendence.

~

All heavenly and earthly creatures are fundamentally linguistic entities that need to be read.

~

Letters contain a hiddenness. We are unable to reveal their secret unless we acknowledge their penchant for silence. Silence is also an aspect of discourse: letters do not have to be uttered.

~

We are called to thought by letters and their arrangement into words. Nothing exists outside this calling. To think is to pronounce.

~

I have spoken of T as a cross for martyrs, as well as a tau for pilgrims on the Way. Death and transcendence find their origin in this simple letter. No man knows when his own talismanic letter will call him to the other side. A tree, a crossbow, these all figure large in such a consonant. It has the feeling of a tomb, and of harpies hovering above. Or are they angels? I am made aware that we are in the hands of small gods who bear the ruffled feathers of our lives. Yes, we do long to fly, in spite of the disorder of our plumes.

~

Do certain words delight us with their discombobulations? I think of the word 'wow!', such a declamatory statement of awe, even wonder. And yet, if we turn it upside down we find ourselves gazing at 'mom', a surprisingly nurturing word. It begs the question, of course: is surprise the mother of all inquiry? A word that makes no sense, is little more than an exhalation, suddenly finds itself giving birth to a timeless spirit of inquiry.

~

Then do we see the Lapis, that unearthed tablet from Cumae, sibyl-talk from a fissure of smoke in Delphi. This is the alchemy of language and earth's claim on our psyche, whereby letters are molded from black soil. This is the call of words in their primal shape: artifice, vultures tearing at flesh during a sky burial on a mountainside in Tibet, so that a troubled soul might be released. Words are the voice of the Spirit yearning to find a homeland. Insects in a termite mound, ever sensitive to the heat of the sun, their bellies filled with digested leaves and debris, these industrious creatures announce the emergence of new thoughts at noon, when the sun is at its zenith. This is the word, this is the vibration of the alphabet as it heats up. Only then is earth and thought made one.

~

Letters, I now realize, are earth's gift to humankind. They lie in furrows, there to take root and sprout. The grain of life flourishes when words and utterance coalesce. Thoth knew this when he patrolled the levee-banks before each harvest seeking nutriment through his beak. In truth, this harvest is one of love and of the miracle of expression. Life is contained in its husk. When waters flood the fields, so does love blossom as a prelude to the healing art of bread. We are in the presence of a master baker who kneads letters into words.

~

If I were, by some miracle, able to create the twenty-seventh letter in the alphabet, I would allow it to adopt the sound of water over rapids. Such a sound would be that of nature yearning to cleanse the soul of the world of all its imperfections. Letters, after all, make up its essence, so that one more addition to the alphabet might better serve nature in its adjudications.

~

Nature, and thus humankind, are all made up of an infinitude of letters. Through them, nature and ourselves tumble into being.

~

On a lacquer tray the five vowels of the alphabet rest like chowan bowls in preparation for a tea ceremony. It is said that once warmed they cool very slowly. Each vowel, perfectly glazed and fired, embodies stillness, elegance, and probity. The sounds they make are filled with their allegiance, as well as their loyalty to the mouth. We sip from each letter nothing less than the obliquity of their taste. Five is a sacred number. It represents oddness, inclusion, and the importance of ceremony as an adjunct to the acquisition of sagacity or knowledge. These vowels are to words what wind is to sails. They fill them with vigor, give direction and energy to the sailing forward of all that constitutes meaning.

~

I note that the fourth century monk Evagrius Ponticus supported himself as a calligrapher while he lived in the Nitria Desert of Egypt. One senses that he wrote in a celestial language. Each letter that he compiled became self-formative, a gathering unto himself. There were practical consequences also: if someone was bitten by an insect, he recommended that a prayer be recited over a bowl of water and then consumed. It seems that words, when mixed with water, became an antidote to inadvertent poisons.

~

Words possess power. This is why, in a past age, the recitation of spells was so potent. "Just recite," the hermit Poemen wrote. "The devil is unable to repel the force of words." Even beasts, he tells us, understand their authenticity and submit. Such is the power of recitation and prayer.

~

Words are intoxicating eddies. They swirl around me like the Great River flowing towards the sea. It is a river of words, the gush of un-announced gold, that high effluvium of distant summits. In a nearby field a stone turtle is lodged, leftover carving of some lost paragon. Words congregate on its shell. They are the sayings of sages who only mimic slowness when they talk. This is because they regard words as the apogee of eggshells, broken easily if not treated with cordiality and respect. I live with their consequence. I become the interpreter of epithets whose origins are redolent of words carved on ancient steles at the border between kingdoms. 'Let no man pass who is not a true emissary of language', they remark in a multiple of idioms. They alone bear the word as a vertical line of letters, signifying ascent and descent.

~

'Pyx'[3] is a strange word. vowel. As with a number of words in English, it has adopted Y as a substitute vowel. Why? Because of its Greek origin? Who knows. But I note that it is often closely associated with X in many other words. Lynx or Styx, for example. I suspect that the metaphysics of Y find comfort in the transcendental nature of X. They are letters in league with one another. Like diamonds these consonants have been fashioned under extreme pressure, and for the sake of translucency. They glitter when closely aligned. At once the vowel 'I' kneels before them, does honour to the combined mystery that they contain.

~

Near the Acacas Mountains in North Africa, in a cave, I came upon desert animals as rock paintings. They reminded me of prehistoric letters migrating across the Serengeti Plains. Yes, I told myself, animals on the move are more than a sequence of paragraphs – those zebra, wildebeest, gazelle and giraffe. The

---

4 Pyx is a container in which the consecrated bread of the Eucharist is kept. In Greek, it means 'box'.

mournful art of displacement: jackals in packs, lions and their prides, the predatory nature of language when it is preparing to hunt.

~

Then there are nouns, posterior to things. I clasp them in my hands. Why is touch so important to language? We touch things. When we caress with our fingers over the weathered surface of a gravestone, we touch death. None of us knows what it is like to feel a palimpsest staring at us from its blank page. Letters erased. Letters lost. Text that no longer speaks to us.

~

Some words seem more evocative than what they represent. 'Horse', for example, is no more than a sign. 'Bird', also. But the word 'armadillo' is filled with suggestion – of an ancient animal struggling to remain relevant. 'Crocodile' is another. When we arrive at 'butterfly', however, we experience a strange sensation – of a slow-melting goldenness and the exhilarating levity of birds. We are entranced, just as we are when we hear the word 'escutcheon'. At this point we are confronted by something indecipherable, a word that goes beyond heraldry to represent the complex arrangement of patterns on war shields, pennants, ship's colours at masthead, and baldachins. The medievalism of language: Old English is a reliquary; it contains words encased in silver, a sheen of indubitable meanings now verdigreed by time. Become a verbal archeologist then, dig up lost meanings, restore them to the sensibility of our age.

~

Words enjoy a certain habitation. There are mansion words, which partake of clipped accents and the sonority of privilege. Café words are more fluid, unstated, not wishing to compete with the sound of coffee cups or the rustle of newspapers. A third type of word enjoys wandering, losing itself in the open air. Instinctively words are drawn to where they belong.

~

And, yes, there are mystical words. These inhabit a more rarified space. Antique books in monastery libraries, temple precincts with elaborate bookstands or prayer wheels which echo the solicitude of monks. I have heard such words reverberate around church cupolas, grazing against mosaics, absorbing the glimmer of countless tesserae. Words of the spirit are more elevated than others – they float above us, caught up in a winged environment, a singular ladder leading everywhere and nowhere.

~

John of Ruusbroec, a medieval Flemish mystic, spoke of a tiny stone called a calculus, which he chose to identify with the Logos. The stone was small underfoot, almost unnoticeable, but capable of spurring a man into action. Used in a rudimentary abacus by merchants in the East, a calculus was thus an instrument of computation. The Logos becomes a form of 'measure', and so both word and number combined. Man as measure of all things in relation to the Christos, perhaps?

It is at this point that language begins to merge with the transcendent. The stone (calx) 'calculated' the rise of the Logos in man. Clearly John of Ruusbroec wanted to find a proto-symbol that would resist the depredations of time, and so become eternal. His calculus, he tells us, is 'fiery red and white', the colours of blood (martyrdom) and the white of redemption. He seems to be saying that language cannot be crushed underfoot, nor can it do anything other than measure the eternal nature of the Logos.

Nature (stone) became the Rock upon which his church was built. For John, a tiny stone was transformed into the gravel through which a man might be aggravated towards the discovery of his eternal nature.

~

In a little book, unfinished at his death, the French writer René Daumal tells the story of a certain M. Sogol who attempts to sail to a remote island on which a summit, Mount Analogue, is located. I am at once alerted to the strange juxtaposition of words. In particular, the name of M. Sogol as a reversal of the word Logos, as well as the mountain that he wishes to climb becoming the 'same as' (ana-logue) of himself. What is Daumal trying to tell us? That the Word is a mysterious and unassailable summit? Until we reverse our dismissive attitude towards the miracle of language, he seems to be saying, we will forever be at the mercy of aggravations caused by the gritty nature of a calculus.

~

A Wordsmith. What, or who is he? Such a person is a maker of words, a poetis. He forges them into subjects of extreme utility and beauty. James Joyce spoke of it when he announced his obligation to become a 'smithy of his soul'. This is the talk of a supreme logomath, a man who sees reality only through the lens of words. Logos - that is, principled reason and imagination - are the tools of a wordsmith. He forges a new reality with language.

The twenty-six letters of the alphabet are thus hammered into words. Bellow and flame causes them to glow in the name of expression.

~

Victor Segalen wrote in his metaphysical tale, Paintings, 'The surface is broken. Here we are on the other side of the earth. But not in blackness; we are following the Path of the Soul into the heart of the monument.' To do so involves the use of the intellect married to words. The soul is a 'radiant darkness', so John of Ruusbroec tells us. And language is the only light capable of penetrating that mound, that darkness. Two men, Victor Segalen and John of Ruusbroec, though centuries apart, have shown us the way: language is soul-stuff, and we the sole beneficiary of its metaphysic.

In Upper Egypt, on the Nile, I met a monk in a monastery who, when I recited a dream to him, offered to translate its meaning for me. "'Put no more wood on the fire,' which you heard a voice saying to you, was a call to change your ways. The fire is your life, and you are constantly inflaming it with illusions and diversions. Let the fire die down, become embers." The anagram had spoken to me through this monk, in a distant place, and language had penetrated my dreams. Since then, my life has become ashes.

~

Wherever the Pantocrator goes he carries a book under his arm. It contains four books within, each one relating a different version of himself. Which does he prefer? The story of his mysterious birth, or those telling of his journeys as a child; ones perhaps of his teaching and miracles, or those depicting his martyrdom? Four lives embraced by a mandala, it seems: the circle within a square. This man savors of incense and ashes. He is a walking flame, sandal-wood in a censor emitting an exquisite perfume. He embodies the limber disposition of a god, as well as the slender frame of a man possessed. More than anything, he wants to show us how to conquer our personhood. The journey he recommends to the other side is more than a word-game, however; it is a laying aside of all that is conceivable in favor of that dark radiance John of Ruusbroec speaks of.

~

We never consider the alphabet as a skin of our thought. It clothes us even though we are naked. The hard carapace of a turtle shell is as nothing when compared to the epidermal textuality of words. They lay upon us the pure vitality of being. They slip into our thoughts with all the suavity of velvet. Let us accept their ipseity, their fullness. The journey of the mind is through the land of words. We are tethered by them outside a nomad's tent, awaiting the moment of flight. Galloping hooved, ah! – the sound of punctuation on the plain.

~

As coral spore in their millions, so does the alphabet spore millions of words. Gestures of the deep find their echo in the way we communicate. The floating ecstasy of words drift over the reef of our minds, a symphony of aqueous life. All gods participate in this apotheosis; their radiance lingers in the shimmering apodictic of letters finding form and meaning in those eddies that finally coalesce into words. Hermes is said to be no more than a herm by the roadside, but he is also a piece of coral inserted into our thoughts.

~

In the Jewish Zohar it is said that Moses, when he entered a glorious cloud, found himself surrounded by angels. He encountered one flaming angel whose eyes and wings emitted sprays of fire. The angel wanted to devour him, such was its incandescence. It was only when Moses uttered the sacred Name pertaining to twelve letters of the Hebrew alphabet that the angel displayed fear. Furthermore, the letters of the alphabet, we are told, are capable of flight). This story suggests that even angels are beholden to the syllables we all share. They are borne aloft on seraphic wings.

~

The pure prima material of words, in their inestimology, becomes the basis of all poetry. Their dense matter outdoes all that possessed by the periodic elements. They resist transformation, and yet intimate at it nonetheless.

~

In the Upanishads we hear various sages and speakers decompose and then recompose words before joining them together in new ways to suggest new relationships. This re-arrangement charges them with power. Such an act incites us to rise above mere verbal understanding and dexterity. It opens the way for us to create new words as our consciousness slowly evolves.

~

Beneath the perceptible form of words a silent essence is hidden. This essence informs every word, and makes it real. One could

*associate 'silent essence' with Al Tirmidhi's 'lights', which he
tells us invades and is part of all words. I begin to suspect that
sound draws its ordering power from this silent essence so that
words might come into existence.*

~

*Words enthrone themselves, giving of themselves to all parts as
to the sum.*

~

*The Phoenix has to be the talisman of letters. Only they are
capable of being transformed by the self-immolation of words.*

~

*'Rose' is one of the most beautiful words in any language. It is
redolent with timeless beauty and yet so fragile, transient. We
revere it as a heraldic device, and lay it at the foot of headstones.
Rilke celebrated the rose in a Muzot graveyard, and Gertrude*

Stein invested it with dignity in one of her more memorable epithets.[4] And yet, few have recognized what 'rose' secretly harbours deep in the folds of its petals. When the letters are re-arranged we are left with the god, Eros. Is this why we love such a bloom? Is it touched by the sacred?

~

The final Decretal of Latters. Each syllable is sacrosanct. They have been given to us by the gods. It is their way of imbuing in us the power of communication with them. Down on your knees, pray for their continued inheritance as the Word.

O

25th June, 2018 Bangalow

---

[5] Cf. Rilke: "Rose, oh pure contradiction/desire to be Nobody's sleep/under so many lids."